# Rebirth

## Taylor Sapp

Alphabet Publishing

# Contents


Before You Read          IV

Rebirth          1

Glossary          16

After You Read          18

Writing          20

# Before You Read

1. Will cloning ever be possible?

2. Should cloning be allowed?

3. Would you like to be cloned?

# Rebirth

José stared at the body of his girlfriend, Liza.

He wanted to get his girlfriend's opinion of the card he held in his hand, but he couldn't reach her. Liza had been in a terrible car accident.

The doctors had tried to save her, but she was too badly hurt. She looked like she was asleep. José wished she could wake up, but he knew that she wouldn't. She didn't have much time left.

The doctors had let him into her room so he could say goodbye. José leaned down to hug her. That's when he noticed a black card on her chest. He picked it up. It said REBIRTH on one side in big white capital letters. On the other side, there was a street address. Above that, small elegant letters read "Cloning: fast and discreet".

He didn't know who had put it there and he didn't care. He knew Liza would disapprove. But José wanted her back anyways.

The day after Liza passed away, José visited the address. The office was clean and modern. A young woman sitting at the desk introduced herself as Camila, a cloning technician. Her voice was soft and kind as she explained the process. She listened as he told her about Liza and then he gave her some paperwork to sign.

Camila signed into the hospital database to read Liza's case. "Would you like us to make any changes?" she asked.

"Excuse me?" he said, confused.

"Looking at her genes, she has a high risk of cancer after the age of 40. We can fix that."

José was still recovering from Liza's death. This stuff about genes was confusing, so he just said, "No, I want her just like before,".

Camila had seen this before. She looked at him and said, "Are you sure?"

José paused. "Wait a minute, how do you know she will get cancer?"

"With new technology, we can read genes, that is DNA, very well. She's also at risk for diabetes."

"And you can fix that?"

"Absolutely. Preventing disease is our most common request to change."

"What other changes can you make?" José couldn't help wanting to know more.

"Genes affect a lot of physical characteristics: your height, eye color, hair color, the shape of your face, how long your eyelashes are, your nose shape, even your weight. You don't want to do too much, but lots of people make small changes."

"You can make her taller?" Liza had always hated being five feet tall. She always wanted to be normal size.

"What about personality issues? It looks like she has a slightly higher-than-average temper."

José was silent for a minute. Then he said, "This is a lot to decide. I wish she were here to give her opinion."

Camila put her hand on his shoulder and smiled gently. "I know this can be a bit odd. If it helps, we have a package deal. It's called the Tune-Up. It will automatically erase any serious problems in her genes and improve her physical or personality characteristics that are considered below-average."

José nodded.

"Trust me, she's going to love being taller, healthier, more attractive and having a better character" Camila said, "This will change your life forever!"

• • • ❂ • ❂ • ❂ • • •

One week later, all was back to normal, sort of. The clone of Liza acted just like the real Liza. The memory of her illness and death had been edited out so she thought she was the original. As far as she knew, she'd suffered minor injuries and been in the hospital for a few hours.

It was hard to hide that she was 5 foot 6 inches now. They hadn't made any big changes to her face or body, but there were a lot of small things that really added up. She'd always been good looking, but now she glowed. Her face was more even, her hair was a bit thicker, and her skin was a little clearer. She looked as if she had a filter from a photo app on her at all times!

José felt very lucky. He had hated the idea of living without her. Almost losing her made him appreciate her even more. He was grateful to have the extra time. He definitely appreciated how attractive she was. She seemed a bit kinder and smarter and funnier too.

However, there was one problem. He wasn't sure if she appreciated him. Would Liza start noticing his little flaws the way he noticed all her positives? What if he got sick in middle-age while she stayed healthy. Would she want to take care of him? What if she decided she could get a new boyfriend, one who was taller and better-looking than him?

Even though Liza treated him the same, José couldn't stop worrying. He stopped sleeping well. Of course, that made him more anxious. Then he would snap at her. She would snap back and he would worry that she hated him. And so on. Then in the middle of the night, he woke up with a solution!

· · · · •·• · · ·

The next day, José was back at the Rebirth Center and meeting with Camila, the same technician. This time he wanted to create his own better clone.

Camila told him, "You are still alive. When we clone a living person, we retire the original."

"What does that mean?"

"We take a sample of your DNA. We put you to sleep and create your clone. Once the clone is ready. We end your life. We just put a poisonous gas in with the sleeping gas. You won't feel anything. Your clone won't even know."

"What?! Why would you do that?" José was horrified.

"It's illegal to have more than one copy of a person alive at the same person. It is too easy to use clones in very bad ways." Camila explained.

"OK. But will I have the same memories?"

"Yes," Camila said, "You'll be just like Liza. You will think you are the original. You won't even remember coming here. You will barely notice a difference. Remember we are only fixing small things so Liza won't know you are a clone. You'll be an half an inch taller. Your skin will be nicer and your eyes will be more shiny, we can make your hair brighter, things like that. We'll also improve your temper a bit. And keep you from going bald."

José had to think carefully for a few minutes. But he couldn't think of a good reason not to do it.

"Ok, go for it."

Camila pressed a button on the wall. "This won't take long. We can get your DNA and take care of you right now."

José lay down on the table, ready to be reborn. The doctor came in and put a mask on him. The mask was attached to some tanks.

"Don't worry. This won't take long. You'll fall asleep and the new you will wake up a few hours from now!"

José started to feel anxious, but it was too late. He was getting sleepy, very sleepy, his eyes closed and his mind went blank.

Suddenly, he realized he was awake. Still tired, he opened his eyes, expecting to see the room where they grow clones. But he was in the same office. The doctor was gone but Camila was there, staring at him. She had a tablet computer on her desk, some kind of file open on it.

"Wait. Why do I remember this?" he said.

Camila didn't answer. She looked confused. She didn't know what to say.

José put his hands on his stomach and noticed it was still chubby. "Hey, I thought you were going to fix this!"

"José, listen carefully." Camila said. "We told you that you can't have more than one clone. But our system says you've been cloned before."

"What?" José didn't understand.

Camila sighed. "This doesn't happen very often. You don't remember, of course."

"Well....no." José's head was spinning. What did this mean? He was a clone?

"That's why we always check. We uploaded your DNA to the national cloning database. That is how we found out." Camila said.

"But, that means there's another me?" José asked.

"I'm not supposed to say anything. But I understand. This is upsetting." Camila said.

"I though that was illegal."

"It is," Camila said, "I don't know how this happened."

"Do you know who cloned me?"

Camila looked at the tablet.

"Wait, is that my file?" José asked. "I want to see it."

"I can't show you the file," Camila said.

"Please!" José begged. "I have to know who I am. I have to know why I'm a clone."

Camila paused for a minute. Then she quickly wrote an address down on a piece of paper.

"I really shouldn't do this," she said, handing him the paper. "This is the address of the original you. He...you ...he has the answer. But ..."

José was starting to get up. He was ready to go see the original him. But he turned to face her again. "What?"

"Well," Camila said, "You, the original you, had a reason for making you. This was your own decision, the original you, I mean. Maybe you should trust yourself."

José laughs. "Trust who?"

"Listen, You can go to that address. It may help you get a few answers. But what I really think you should do is go and enjoy your life."

"How can I enjoy my life when I don't know who I am?" José turned and left the office.

· · · ● · ● ● · · ·

He put the address in his phone's map app. The directions took him a very nice neighborhood. The houses looked big. A lot of them were behind fancy walls. The yards were enormous.  The address he was looking for had a gate. There was a camera and speaker next to the gate. A tough-sounding voice asked for his name, then told him to look right at the camera. After a short time, the gate swung open. José drove up the long drive past beautiful trees and gardens. He came to a huge mansion. He parked between a Bentley and a Ferrari.

He walked up to the main door. It was already open. There was a man standing in the doorway. The man was probably 80 years old, but he looked a lot like José.

"So you're the real José?" he asked.

"My name is Luis, actually. I'm impressed, José. You're the first one to find me."

Luis invited José in. His servant served them coffee outside in the backyard. José could see a pool, a hot tub, a tennis court, and a beautiful rose garden.

"It's funny how you look just like me. Other things are different. You sit with your knees apart. I always sit knees together. And you put more sugar in your coffee than me." Luis was studying him carefully.

José was impatient "Tell me what's going on. Isn't this illegal? I'm a clone of you, but you're still alive!"

Luis laughed. "Rebirth is my company. That's how I got so rich. It also means no one submits my DNA when I make a clone."

"But why did you clone yourself? Why are you still alive? Why don't I remember being you?" José asked.

"You're not my final clone. You are part of the test group."

"The test group?"

"I want to create the perfect clone. I need to test how different changes to DNA work out. So I made a lot of clones. Each has slightly different DNA edits. I learned to make a clone that never gets sick! My new clone is also very fit and strong. I will be a super man."

"So what does that mean for me?" José asked.

"Most of my clones are better than average. You said your name is José?" Luis asked.

"Yes," José replied.

"Are you a teacher?

"Yes, how did you know?"

"I gave each clone a different name. It helps me keep track of you all. I made you with extra genes for caring about others. I'll bet you are the best teacher at your school."

It was true. José was teacher of the year almost every year at school. He had a popular blog and a big social media following, too. He had even won state and national awards for teaching.

"I can see it on your face. See? You have nothing to complain about," Luis said. "All my clones have great lives. They have good jobs or happy families or interesting hobbies. One is an Olympic athlete. Another is a famous actor."

"It feels wrong though. You have a chance no one else has."

"That's the caring part of you talking. I am 80 years old and I have lung cancer. I have one year left. Why shouldn't I want the best for myself?"

"What will happen when you die?"

"My new super clone is almost ready. They will give it my memories. I will be just like Liza. Yes, I read your file. Don't be shocked!"

"But what will happen to us, your other clones, when you die?"

"Nothing. I told you that you are the first to figure it out. I don't think anyone else will."

"Maybe I will find the other clones and tell them."

"That will create problems for me. After all, what I am doing is illegal. So I have an idea. I am very rich. You deserve a reward for finding out the truth? I will give you a million dollars if you forget about our little conversation…"

It struck José that it all seemed a little too easy. "I'm not the first to come here, am I?"

Luis laughed again. "You're also not the first to say exactly that!"

José was angry and confused. He stood up and said, "I don't need your money. I don't want to be part of your game."

Suddenly, Luis looked at him very seriously. "I can use my money to hurt you too. I can bribe your principal to fire you. I can buy your apartment building and kick you out. When I get my new body, I can beat you up, even kill you. I suggest you take the money and go."

· · · · ● · ● · · ·

When José got home, Liza was sitting on the couch, looking worried. "Where were you?" she asked. It's late and you didn't text or call."

"Sorry. There was an event at school. I thought I told you."

"But why didn't you answer my texts? I was worried." Liza sounded upset.

José had to tell her the truth. "You're not going to believe this. I met someone today."

He told her the whole story.

She listened carefully. She didn't say anything. She didn't interrupt. José didn't know if Liza believed him.

Then she asked one question.

Near the end, she stopped him and said, "Did you take the money? Are we rich? Or are we in danger?"

José smiled and said ...

# Glossary

bribe: money paid to someone for them to do something bad

chubby: a bit overweight, slightly fat

clone: an exact copy of a living thing. Currently cloning humans is likely impossible and illegal in the US

diabetes: a disease where your body cannot process sugar properly

discreet: careful, without telling a lot of people

DNA: a collection of genes

flaws: mistakes or problems

genes: a part of your DNA. Genes help determine what living things look and act like

glowed: got bright with light

horrified: full of shock and fear

keep track of: collect information about some-thing over a period of time

rebirth: coming back to life, born again

snap: (here) to say something with anger

tanks: large metal or glass containers often filled with liquid

technician: a person who operates complicated equipment

# After You Read

1. What is Rebirth and what does it do?

2. How does José use Rebirth for Liza?

3. Why does José decide to use Rebirth for himself?

4. What does José learn about himself?

5. How does he react to that news?

6. Who is Luis and what does he have to do with Rebirth

7. What offer does Luis make to José?

8. Do you agree with José's decision to clone Liza?

9. Do you agree with his decision to clone

himself?

10. Do you think Luis' decision to test different clones is wrong?

11. Do you think Luis has a secret plan he didn't tell José?

12. What would you do if you were José?

# Writing

Write the rest of the story.

- What does José say?

- Did he take the money or not?

- What happens to José and Liza?